The Beating of Wings

Story
Emmet O'Cuana

Artwork
Jeferson Sadzinski

Lettering & Design
Thomas Mauer

Cover
Tim Molloy

SNF
SNF
SNF

LAZARUS-MEN.
CORPSES THAT
WALK. RAISED BY
THE MAGUS TO
HUNT SINNERS.

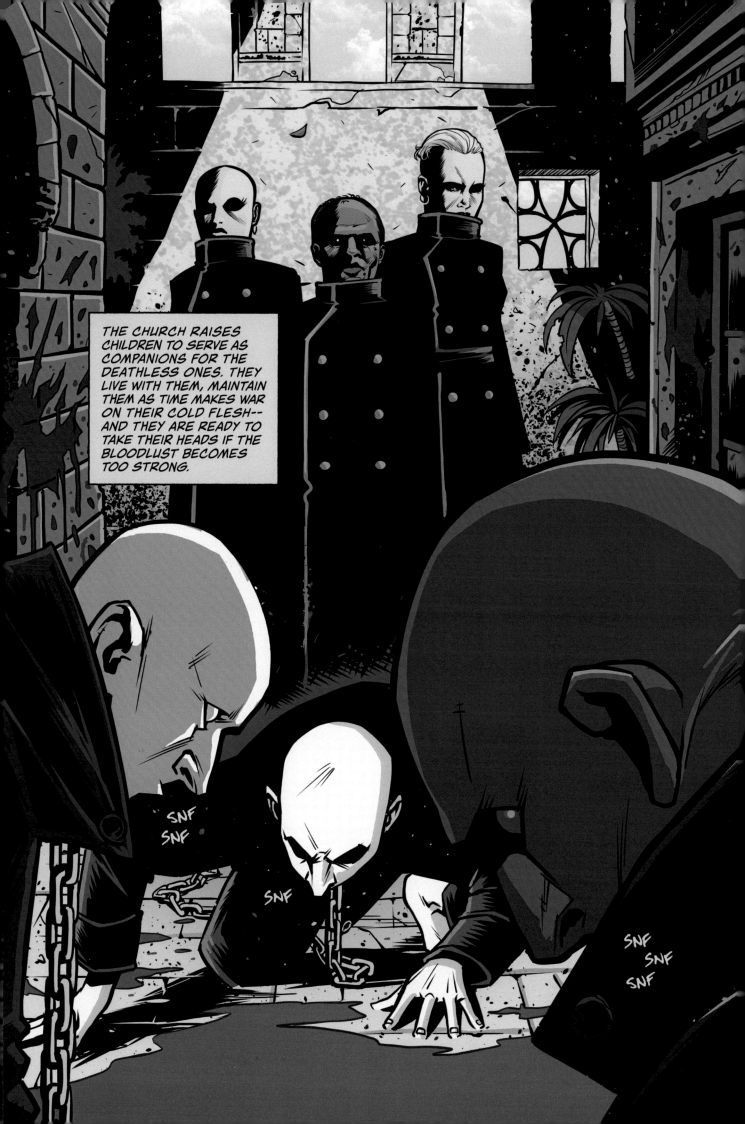

YOU THINK YOU ARE HOME. SAFE.

Elsewhere.

Gallery

Aisling King-Macklin

Laura Renfrew

Sarah Winifred Searle

Brother December.

He has served since he was but a boy.

As his body aged, and his memory drifted,
he began to worry that he would soon be of no use.

That he would no longer be able to serve.

And at night, in the dark quiet spaces,

the spirits would whisper to him of a life neverending.

All it would cost is his soul.

Artist
Aisling King-Macklin

Gotha succeeded, and surpassed, Brother December
shortly after she took holy orders.

She is the fire that burns brightest in Emmanuel.

The Magus keeps a close eye on her progress.

The world favours the strong, the vital and determined.

Sister Gotha will ride the storm that comes.

Pity those weaker souls caught in her wake.

Artist
Laura Renfrew

Rebecca of Tarsus. That was her name.

The first Magus.

The first to see that this world is surrounded

by many worlds, ideas of worlds, and yes, hells.

No heaven above or damnation below but on all sides

every kind of life and unlife teams and seeks to spread,

an infinity of existence.

Rebecca of Tarsus looked, she saw,
she gained knowledge of countless worlds

and they looked back.

Artist
Sarah Winifred Searle

Wings of Desire
(the desire to make this comic)

The best way to start an afterword is to thank the reader – so thank you, reader, whoever you are. I hope you enjoyed this 'fantasy horror' romp by Jeff, Thomas and myself. I'll get back to those lads shortly, but first –

Thank you, Stevie. Thanks for smiling at me every morning. Thanks for your laughter. Thanks for kicking my arse so that I make things, like this comic, and put them out into the world. None of this happens without your smile, your laughter, your kindness (and the occasional boot up the hole!).

I have more thanks to give, and I will below, but first a story.

In 2003 I was working as a waiter in the Royal Museum of Scotland. I had moved to Edinburgh to join my college friend Aengus, who needed a flatmate to help pay bills. And with our combined financial worth we...barely scraped by honestly. In fact, while the monthly wages from my work went towards rent, it was my practice of stealing soup from the restaurant that kept me alive. 'The time of soup', is how Aengus and I describe those months, when a packet of store-brand Bourbon biscuits was the height of luxury.

But still this was one of the happiest times of my life. Now the job of being a waiter was a miserable one, working away with the dull dead eyes of Dolly the Sheep in her glass display case watching me take abuse from American tourists at my difficult to understand accent. Still the memories that rise to the surface are happy ones.

There was the time I served a table where a literary scholar from Pakistan and a Palestinian activist were seated together. When the scholar heard me speak, he excitedly reeled off an anecdote about James Joyce mentioning the Indian revolution against the British in *Ulysses*. Then he turned to the young woman from Palestine and said "We three are all rebels together!" It was one of the few times in my life that I felt connected to something bigger than myself, a sense of community based in an alternate telling of history opposed by occupation and invasion narratives.

The other key memory I have is how I would spend time between work and home in the Edinburgh Central Library. I would enter, grab as many books my membership would allow me to take, and then mosey on home to Inverleith Gardens weighed down by the dozen or so tomes in my bag.

And that was how I discovered Frances Yates, and by a long and winding road, came to write *The Beating of Wings*.

Frances Yates was a religious historian with a very accessible style of writing, that nonetheless rests on rigorous and in-depth research. My introduction to her was her book *Giordano Bruno and the Hermetic Tradition*. Bruno was a member of the Dominican order who, seemingly inspired by an early interest in Thomas Aquinas, pursued a study of religious philosophy. This in turn led to his becoming a proponent of the theory that Christianity had suppressed ancient Egyptian religious ideas. Bruno was arguing in favour of a return to a form of religion that embraced magical systems similar to cabalism. He saw Copernicus's idea that the sun was orbited by the earth as proof of an even greater truth – that there are many worlds and our existence continues in many forms, both spiritual and physical.

For his trouble, Bruno was burned at the stake after being arrested in 1591. Yates investigates his life with a sense of compassion and curiosity that is very compelling. Reading her in 2003 I found her presentation of ideas and research thrilling. I've said before in an interview in Aurealis magazine in 2013 that I think I fell in love with her a bit. I only later discovered she died the year I was born.

Her championing of Bruno was intoxicating. His campaign to unify the different faiths carving up 16th century Europe in wars and conflict – it's important to remember how inextricably linked religion and politics were in this time; we should not return to the same sources of division so eagerly – by proselytising in favour of magical practice stayed with me.

Bruno's big idea seems to me that magic forces us to regard the spiritual as an everyday reality. The priest speaking to a congregation about the spiritual life rests on dogmatic assertions. There is no doing, only recitation. Bruno used magic to bundle up religion, philosophy, maths and memory. 'Practical magic' for all people is what I think was his point.

And I should address another concern here, my own feelings on religion. Basically, my stance is – faith is a wonderful thing. I don't have it, but I am happy for those that do. I worked for an Australian church for three years because my role allowed me to help vulnerable members of the community in wider Victoria connect online. I would build congregation websites so church members could interact more widely. I see the value in religious practice as a function of social gathering, a tool to navigate our existence here on Earth.

But for myself, to paraphrase a Sue Townsend line, 'like all atheists I love churches'. I am fascinated by religious history and philosophy. The Christian religion is a continuing filter for how I experience the world. It would be silly for me to deny how fundamental its influence on me is; still, I choose not to believe.

Needless to say, Yates and her research stayed with me, but mainly as a fond memory of a summer spent reading books because I could not afford to do anything else. The library in Edinburgh gave me hope and enjoyment when I was counting my pennies and debating the cost of taking the bus over walking across town.

My brief research into Hermetic magick is the colour, the grit in the oyster shell, for *The Beating of Wings*. But Yates and Bruno and all that really exists only here in this essay. The script itself for *The Beating of Wings* was an exercise. It was me sitting in another library on the other side of the world, writing down panel descriptions in a copybook, for the sake of an artistic collaborator to just go nuts with demons and the undead. I pitched the script to editor John Schork as C.S. Lewis' *A Horse And His Boy* meets *Hellraiser*. John's kind feedback and encouragement gave me confidence in what I had written.

Cheers mate, I hope we see you in this part of the world again.

I did not dare to hope Jeff would be available to work on this, but I was delighted when he agreed.

Jeferson Sadzinski, and Thomas Mauer, worked with me previously on my fantasy one-shot *Faraway*, a silly little story about wizards and a dreaming child. This book in your hands is probably the last time we will be working together as a team. A career in comics is a tenuous thing, and these two lads are on to greener pastures.

But look at what Jeff has done here. The "nighthaunts" in all their demonic glory manage to sketch winged devils and Max Schreck's Nosferatu. Then there's the Lazarus-men, essentially consecrated zombies employed by these magic-practicing priests (the malign narrator's mention of December and his peers stealing the language

a

The BEATING OF WINGS.

b

THE BEATING OF WINGS

c

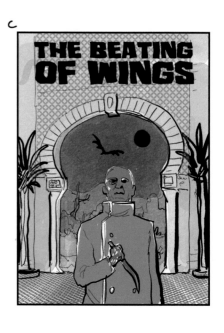

THE BEATING OF WINGS

d

THE BEATING OF WINGS.

e

THE BEATING OF WINGS.

BONE AND MEAT DIMENSION?
← FLESH CREEPING ALLOVER THE Arabesque Patterns on the interior—RED LIT HELL

f

THE BEATING OF WINGS

g

The beating of wings

h

THE BEATING OF WINGS

i

THE BEATING OF WINGS

RUBBLE/SKULL ↑

of angels is a nod to Gnosticism); Gotha a character I left to Jeff to invent based on a short description of a tall, domineering woman, and he created something approximate to a demon-slaying Annie Lennox (and everyone I approached to produce a standalone illustration wanted to do their take on Gotha); Emmanuel itself, drawn mostly from a half-remembered school trip to Tunis which here is remade as a fusion of 20th century and Arabian architecture – the eclecticism of style and fine detail is why I have no doubt Jeff is going to take the US comics industry by storm.

Full credit to Thomas too for working hard on the finishing touches to this comic mid-COVID panic and uncertainty. In a comic about language as magic, it's fitting that the letterer should have fashioned *The Beating of Wings* into what it's become. Thomas caught mistakes, gave feedback on the text and delivered his work with consideration and professionalism.

I tragically continue to make jokes about 'an Irishman, a Brazilian and a German walk into a bar', but this is truly an international work, facilitated by the global reach of the internet. I could never have guessed during my topsy-turvy time in Edinburgh just how connected I would one day be to a much wider world.

Of course, it was Australia that has become my home and the community I found here that encouraged me to take up making comics.

As with *Faraway*, I saw this comic as an opportunity to showcase the work of artists I have met or discovered through the local scene.

Laura Renfrew (https://lafrew.carbonmade.com/) is an artist whose work has a joy to it I find irresistible. Try to track down a copy of her book *Blue* if you have a chance. Laura and I first met through the Melbourne comics 'meets', held once every month. She was first to create an accompanying illustration based on the events of this comic and chose to do a profile of Gotha. The result, something so unlike what I expected but entirely in keeping with the alternate-history Byzantinism of *The Beating of Wings*.

One time, Laura and I both served on a panel about Asterix versus Tintin. In memory of that happy day, Up Gaul!

Sarah Winifred Searle (http://www.swinsea.com/) chose to depict the woman who would become the first Magus in this alternate history where magical practice led to a fusion of the three main Abrahamic faiths. I first encountered Sarah at the 2018 Perth Comics Arts Festival (PCAF) held at Edith Cowan university. She spoke from the audience during one of the panels – quite passionately as I recall – and then kindly shared photos on social media from my own talk on Australian superhero comics. It was afterwards that I realized she was the artist on a book I was quite fond of called *Ruined*, as well as *Fresh Romance*. Sarah was puzzled as to why I approached her to work on this book, given its fantasy horror elements, but over the course of our correspondence the idea for 'Rebecca of Tarsus' the first Magus in the 16th century took shape. I couldn't be happier with the result. The style and cut-glass classic look of this illustration is exactly the reason why I approached Sarah in the first place.

As for Aisling King Macklin (https://linktr.ee/aiiisling) I have not met this extraordinary artist of fluid bodies and bleeding phantasmagoria – but needless to say I find her work very compelling. After I reached out, Aisling unprompted began to allude to the work of Austin Osman Spare. Now at the time that I first read about Giordano Bruno, I was still grappling with J.H. Williams III and Alan Moore's *Promethea*. That comic introduced me to the work of Spare, a fascinating person, whose art and magickal practice drew descent from the same Hermetic sources as Bruno's. In discussing Spare, Aisling and

I arrived at the idea of depicting the multiple worlds that overlap with our own that lies behind *The Beating of Wings*. Spare's monstrous angelic creatures, and Aisling's punk surrealism, combine in her vision of December surrounded by spirits and demons.

I feel as if these illustrations dip and duck around the groundwork of Bruno's Hermeticism, just as my script and the finished comic by Jeff and Thomas tease at the ideas behind this alternate history.

The real tantalising element is the incredible cover by Tim Molloy (https://www.timmolloy.com/), a hellworld arabesque. The detail and hints of horror and fantasy trumped my rather long and unwieldy brief. Nevertheless, because he's a professional

(and an artistic machine) Tim pumped out a set of thumbnailed concepts. Any one of them would have been a great cover, but I think we settled on the perfect choice. Tim is someone who I've admired for some time. We bonded over a discussion of David Lindsay's *A Voyage* to *Arcturus*, and here's an intention I'd like to put out into the world. If anyone would be interested in an artistic interpretation of that visionary work – here's your man.

These are the folks who helped me make this comic. As I said before in my afterword for *Faraway*, I would not be able to do this were it not for having a dayjob that both pays household bills, but also allows me to squirrel a little something aside. I see this comic as a passion project as a result, something I can make and put out into the world. I am more than aware that I enjoy a great deal of privilege to be able to afford to do so.

2020 has been at best a difficult year, and for many disastrous. Just as we were learning about the global spread of COVID-19, my father Gerard Cooney passed away in Dublin, Ireland. March became a collapsing black hole of time, of panicked international flights, paranoid fears about infection and health risks, and above all sheer, numbing grief. The months since have extended that sense of unreality. As I type this, Stevie and I are still in lockdown in Melbourne. Opportunists in positions of power and with public platforms are using this disastrous health crisis to further divide the country and entrench fear among communities. It's a bleak, sad time for us all.

I can only say thank you. Thank you to Stevie for helping me get through this year. Thank you to Jeff, Thomas, John, Laura, Sarah, Aisling and Tim for all their fine work – you all gave me something bright to look forward to with every email exchange and message. Thanks dad, for giving me stories.

And thank you for reading this.

We're all rebels together.

Emmet O'Cuana,
Melbourne, September 2020

BONE AND MEAT DIMENSION?

← FLESH CREEPING ALL OVER THE ARABESQUE PATTERNS ON THE INTERIOR - RED LIT HELL

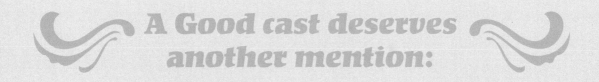

A Good cast deserves another mention:

Emmet O'Cuana

Emmet O'Cuana is a Dublin-born, regional Victoria-based writer and critic. He is also an aspiring home cook. One day, he dreams of owning a miniature goat.

emmetocuana.com

Jeferson Sadzinski

Jeferson Sadzinski is a comic book artist from Curitiba in Brazil. His interest in sequential art first came from watching cartoons as a child. He still likes to imagine his own stories and draw them in his spare time. Jef has been published by Image Comics and Mad Cave Studios. In 2018, Jef was one of the winners of the 2018 Mad Cave Studios Talent Search.

deviantart.com/jeffsadzinski/gallery
https://jefsadzinski.tumblr.com
Twitter: @JefSadzinski
Instagram: @je.ff.e
Email: jef_sadzinski@hotmail.com

Thomas Mauer

Thomas Mauer has lent his lettering and design talent to numerous critically acclaimed and award-winning projects since the early 2000s. Among his recent work are ComiXology's 40 SECONDS and IN THE FLOOD, Aftershock's MILES TO GO and TKO Presents' LONESOME DAYS, SAVAGE NIGHTS and THE PULL, THE DARK and Image Comics' HARDCORE and THE REALM.

You can follow him on
Twitter @thomasmauer and see samples of his work at www.thomasmauer.com

Tim Molloy

Tim Molloy (New Zealand) makes weird art, mostly in the form of comics and watercolour paintings. He is inspired by the occult, religion, horror, science fiction, psychedelia and a lifetime of bizarre dreams. Tim's award winning 'Mr Unpronounceable' books have garnered a cult following.

https://www.timmolloy.com/

Laura Renfrew – https://lafrew.carbonmade.com
Aisling King-Macklin – https://linktr.ee/aiiisling
Sarah Winifred Searle – http://www.swinsea.com